MEET THE GREATS

Nelson MANDELA

TIM COOKE

Gareth Stevens PUBLISHING

Please visit our website, www.garethstevens.com.
For a free color catalog of all our high-quality books,
call toll free 1-800-542-2595 or fax 1-877-542-2596.

Cataloging-in-Publication Data

Names: Cooke, Tim.
Title: Nelson Mandela / Tim Cooke.
Description: New York : Gareth Stevens Publishing, 2020. | Series: Meet the greats | Includes glossary and index.
Identifiers: ISBN 9781538252499 (pbk.) | ISBN 9781538252505 (library bound)
Subjects: LCSH: Mandela, Nelson, 1918-2013--Juvenile literature. | Presidents--South Africa--Biography--Juvenile literature. | Political prisoners--South Africa--Biography--Juvenile literature.
Classification: LCC DT1974 C66 2020 | DDC 968.06'5092 B--dc23

Published in 2020 by
Gareth Stevens Publishing
111 East 14th Street, Suite 349
New York, NY 10003

Picture crediits: Front cover: Character artwork Supriya Sahai. Interior: Getty Images: Jean-Pierre Muller/ AFP 31, Allan Tannenbaum 28; Public Domain: 9, A Bailey 11, Guinnog 14, ign11 32, Johannesburg Heritage Foundation 10, André Koehne 34, Lysippos 8, Nationa Archief of the Nederlands/Rob C. Croes/Anefo 12, John Pannell 43, rahuldiucca (R. Barraez D'Lucca), 24, 25t, Henry M. Trotter 15t, 39, Witstinkhout 20, Rudiger Wolk 21; Shutterstock: 360b 33, Mike Browne 35t, catwalker 29, 41, fivepointsix 40, Gil K 22, Howard Klaaste 15b, F Meijer-Innes 23, milosk50 30, Sean Nel 42, Marek Poplawski 19,Valentina Proskurina 13, Mark Reinstein 35b, The Old Major 25b, Bart Vos 18, Wandel Guides 38.

Printed in the United States of America

CPSIA compliance information: Batch #CW20GS: For further information contact Gareth Stevens, New York, New York at 1-800-542-2595.

Contents

Introduction

Despite spending 27 years as a political prisoner, Nelson Mandela went on to become South Africa's first black president.

Mandela was sent to prison in 1962 for fighting for the **civil rights** of black South Africans. At the time, the country was governed by a white minority. Black South Africans were kept separate from whites, denied good jobs or education, and excluded even from voting.

During his time in prison, Mandela became a global symbol of fighting against the **apartheid** system in South Africa. When the government gave in to international pressure and released him in 1990, he worked with the then-president F. W. de Klerk to end apartheid. The two men jointly won the Nobel Prize for Peace in 1993. In 1994, Mandela was elected president in the first elections in which black South Africans were allowed to vote. He only served one term, until 1999, but he became a **figurehead** for civil rights and racial equality around the world.

Making TROUBLE

Nelson Mandela's original name meant "troublemaker." It was a sign of the impact he would later have on South Africa.

Nelson Mandela was born Rolihlahla Mandela on July 18, 1918, in a tiny village in Transkei in South Africa. In the language of the Xhosa people, Rolihlahla means "pulling the branch of a tree," but the name is usually translated as "troublemaker." He was also given the **clan** name of Madiba. Mandela's father belonged to the royal family of the Thembu people, but he lost his important social position in a political dispute. The Mandela family moved to an even smaller village, called Qunu. Nelson grew up playing outside with other boys and herding his mother's cattle.

QUICK FACTS

- Nelson was born into a South African royal family and brought up in a palace.
- He ran away to the city of Johannesburg, where he joined the fight for rights for black South Africans.

The university at Fort Hare attracted black students from all over southern Africa.

A NEW NAME

Rolihlahla's mother was a Christian, so she sent him to a school run by Christian **missionaries**. Students at the school had "English" names. On Rolihlahla's first day, his teacher told him he would be called Nelson. He never found out why.

Nelson's father died while Nelson was still at school. His mother took him to be brought up by the Thembu **regent**, Chief Jongintaba Dalindyebo. Nelson moved into Jongintaba's palace. He did well at school by working very hard. In 1939, he enrolled to study for a degree at the University College of Fort Hare, a school for smart black students. He studied law to prepare him for his future career as a royal advisor.

RUNNING AWAY

Nelson became a member of the Student Representative Council, but he resigned his position in a dispute over the poor food in the university. The principal threw him out. Regent Jongintaba was so angry that he decided to take control of Nelson's life. He arranged a marriage for him, which was common in Thembu families.

Mandela panicked. He ran away to Johannesburg, the largest city in South Africa. There, he found work as a security guard while he continued his studies by mail. He then enrolled in the University of Witwatersrand to study law. At the end of the course, he failed to graduate. By then, his life had become dominated by politics.

Nelson Mandela as a teenager.

FIGHTING FOR A SAY

South Africa was ruled by white people, but Mandela heard stories about when Africans ruled themselves, before Europeans had arrived. He enjoyed Thembu royal ceremonies linked to traditions that had survived for centuries. It seemed to Mandela that black South Africans needed more of a say in their government.

In 1944, Mandela joined the African National Congress (ANC). This was a political movement that aimed to fight for the rights of black South Africans. Mandela and his schoolmate, Oliver Tambo, set up a youth league of the ANC to work with young people to prevent **discrimination**.

Johannesburg was an economic center, but most businesses belonged to white South Africans.

The small house where Mandela and Evelyn moved in 1946 is now a museum.

In 1944, Mandela met and married a nurse, Evelyn Mase, who also worked for the ANC. She was the first of his three wives. The couple moved into a house in the **township** of Orlando in Soweto.

DIVIDED BY RACE

South Africa held a general election in 1948 in which only white South Africans were allowed to vote. They elected a **racist** government that introduced a system known as apartheid, or "apartness." It changed the laws to keep white and black South Africans separate. It also limited the rights of blacks to ensure that government remained in the hands of the white minority.

FIGHTING INJUSTICE

Mandela's youth league (ANCYL) came up with a plan to fight the new system. It planned to use nonviolent protest to force the government to give black South Africans full citizenship through **boycotts**, strikes, and **civil disobedience**. These were similar tactics to those Mahatma Gandhi had used to achieve independence for India from British rule. Mandela and Tambo encouraged people not to obey unfair laws. They traveled across the country to organize protests. Meanwhile, Mandela and Tambo also started their own law firm in order to provide low-cost legal advice to black South Africans.

Mandela's friend Oliver Tambo became president of the ANC in 1967 and held the post until 1991.

In all, Mandela faced three major trials in South Africa's courts.

VIOLENT PROTEST

Mandela helped lead protests for over a decade. In 1956, he was among 156 ANC activists who were arrested and charged with treason, or trying to overthrow the government. Eventually they were all found not guilty. The ANC was changing, however. Some members were concerned that nonviolent protest was not working. They believed the ANC needed a more **radical** approach.

Around the same time, Mandela's personal life was changing, too. He and Evelyn had grown apart and divorced. In 1958, he married a social worker and ANC activist named Winnie Madikizela. The couple had two daughters. However, Winnie would have to bring the girls up on her own because Mandela would spend their childhoods in prison.

Divided by RACE

The apartheid system set up in South Africa in 1948 divided the country on racial grounds. It gave far more rights to white South Africans than to blacks.

South Africa was governed as a British **colony** until 1934, when the British allowed it to govern itself. Power remained in the hands of white South Africans, however. Many of these were Afrikaners, who were originally descended from Dutch colonists in South Africa. In 1948, Afrikaner parties won the general election and introduced apartheid to try to protect their privileges.

The new laws divided South Africans into three racial groups: White, African, and Coloured. A fourth category, Asian, was later added to include Indians and Pakistanis.

This apartheid sign is in English, Afrikaans, and the Bantu language.

The Cape Coloured racial group were classed as a subset of the Coloured race.

The races were forced to live separately and were not allowed to marry one another. Public facilities were divided between whites and blacks.

Black South Africans had to carry special passes that would allow them to visit areas reserved for white citizens. Many black workers were forced to live in huge **shanty towns** called townships, which often lacked many services. More than 3.5 million people were forced to move to "tribal homelands," even though they had little connection with them.

Black South Africans faced many restrictions on where they could go.

Political PRISONER

In 1961, the South African government took dramatic steps to end the anti-apartheid campaign of the ANC.

On March 21, 1960, police at Sharpeville township shot dead 69 people in a crowd protesting laws that forced black South Africans to carry **pass books**. The shootings caused outrage. The government banned opposition groups, including the ANC. In 1961, Mandela founded an armed branch of the ANC, called Umkhonto we Sizwe, or MK. It would fight the government with **sabotage** and **guerrilla** war. That same year, Mandela led workers in a three-day strike. He hoped damaging the economy might force the government into changing its policies.

QUICK FACTS

- Nelson became a major leader of the anti-apartheid campaign.
- In 1963, when he was already in prison, he was sentenced to life imprisonment for his political activities.

Robben Island is about 4½ miles (7 km) from mainland South Africa.

ANOTHER TRIAL

The strike was highly effective, but it only made the government more irritated by Mandela's activities. In 1962, he was arrested, put on trial, and sentenced to five years in prison for having led the strike. That was still not long enough for his political opponents, however.

The government was determined to put a stop to the ANC campaign. In 1963, it put 11 of the most important leaders of the organization on trial for a range of political offenses, including sabotage. Mandela was one of the men in the dock, even though he was already in prison. At the end of the trial, the defendants were all found guilty and sentenced to life imprisonment.

A HARSH PRISON

The ANC leaders were sent to Robben Island, off the coast of Cape Town. It had once been a colony for people suffering from the disease leprosy and was now a prison. When the new prisoners got off the boat to begin their sentences, the warden greeted them by saying, "This is the Island. This is where you will die."

To begin with, conditions for the new arrivals were tough. The prisoners each had a concrete cell about 7 feet by 7 feet (2.1 by 2.1 m) in a new block built especially for them. They had to exercise in a small concrete courtyard and were not even allowed anything to read.

Three of the political prisoners sent to Robben Island later became presidents of South Africa.

Mandela's cell had only the most basic pieces of furniture.

MAKING TROUBLE

Mandela was prisoner 46664, meaning he was the 466th person to arrive on Robben Island in 1964. He soon emerged as a leader among the political prisoners. He encouraged them to move slowly when the guards tried to make them run.

Mandela protested about the ill treatment he and his colleagues suffered. He was punished by being kept in solitary confinement, when he was locked into his cell on his own. He later said these times on his own were the worst thing about his period in prison: "There is only one's own mind, which can begin to play tricks."

CONTINUED EDUCATION

Over time, conditions improved slightly. Prisoners were allowed to read books and even to study. Mandela encouraged his fellow prisoners to learn Afrikaans, the language of the Boer rulers of South Africa. He finally completed his own law degree by mail with the University of London. Robben Island came to be nicknamed the "university behind bars."

While Mandela was in prison, his mother died. In addition, his oldest son died in a car crash. The authorities refused to allow him to go to either of the funerals. Meanwhile, Winnie was raising their daughters on her own, without them seeing their father.

Every day, the prisoners had to work in blinding sunshine to crush limestone into gravel in a quarry.

People around the world were horrified at the conditions in which black South Africans lived in townships such as Soweto.

INTERNATIONAL FAME

While Mandela was getting used to the routine in prison, his reputation kept growing. In the early 1980s, a growing international movement emerged to have him released. Mandela became one of the most famous political prisoners in the world. No one even knew what he looked like, however, as he had not been seen outside the prison for over a decade. The cause of the ANC was still attracting international attention. Behind the scenes, the South African government was beginning to accept that it would have to talk to Mandela and the ANC.

TALKING TO THE GOVERNMENT

In 1982, Mandela and other ANC leaders were moved to a prison at Pollsmoor on the mainland. There, Mandela was told that the president, P. W. Botha, had offered to release the political prisoners in return for a promise to give up their armed struggle. The ANC prisoners all signed a letter written by Mandela rejecting the offer.

Over the next years, government officials quietly met with representatives of the ANC. Many of the meetings took place outside South Africa. In 1988, the ANC prisoners were moved again, this time to Victor Verster prison near Cape Town. Mandela had his own cottage, with TV, newspapers, and a radio—and access to a swimming pool. He was allowed to have any visitors he wanted. In 1989, Mandela finally met President Botha face to face in secret.

At Pollsmoor Prison (bottom), Mandela and his colleagues were closer to the center of government.

Free Nelson MANDELA!

In 1984, the English band The Specials released a song called "Free Nelson Mandela!" It became an anthem around the world.

The song became a symbol of an international movement to try to force South Africa to abandon apartheid. The movement echoed attempts within South Africa, where organizations such as student groups, trades unions, and churches continued to arrange protests against the apartheid system.

A bus in London is painted with an anti-apartheid message.

Protestors outside the South African Embassy in London fly the black, green, and yellow flag of the ANC.

From the early 1960s until the early 1990s, individuals in many countries responded to appeals from black South Africans by boycotting goods from South Africa. This meant they stopped buying them. Many academics refused to cooperate with South African institutions. Banks and financial companies stopped investing money in South Africa. The governing bodies of most sports barred teams from competing in or against South Africa because its teams were **segregated**.

Eventually, South Africa was largely isolated on the world stage. It was also left economically weak. This was one of the main reasons the government eventually had to consider changing its apartheid policies.

U.S. students protest links with apartheid South Africa.

A Black PRESIDENT

In 1989, Frederick Willem de Klerk became president of South Africa. He wanted to end the country's international isolation.

The international campaign against apartheid had led to a boycott of sales of South African products around the world. International sports teams refused to come to play. Music stars no longer visited. There were even fears that the country would fall apart in a civil war between whites and blacks.

De Klerk decided he had to give in to pressure. On February 11, 1990, he announced the release of Nelson Mandela and his fellow political prisoners. He also dropped all restrictions on political groups, including the ANC.

QUICK FACTS

- The government released Nelson as part of its moves to end apartheid.
- Nelson was elected president in South Africa's first multiracial general election.

WALK TO FREEDOM

Nelson Mandela walked to freedom that same day, with Winnie at his side. Crowds turned out to greet him. It was a **symbolic** moment that suggested that change was coming to South Africa. If de Klerk hoped the pressure for change would drop, however, he was mistaken. Mandela at once supported the efforts of foreign governments to force South Africa to change the system of apartheid. In 1991, Mandela was elected president of the ANC. He said the organization would continue its armed struggle as long as blacks were discriminated against, although he committed himself to peaceful change.

Nelson Mandela walked out of prison after 27 years, accompanied by his wife Winnie.

This stamp from Micronesia celebrates the roles of de Klerk and Mandela in ending apartheid.

FRAGILE PEACE

The atmosphere was still dangerous. There were outbreaks of violence as Mandela and de Klerk discussed how to end apartheid. The government offered to share power with black South Africans, but some blacks wanted to simply take power. While Mandela tried to keep the ANC united, de Klerk's National Party also split over his proposed changes. The talks became bogged down.

In April 1993, a white right-wing immigrant shot dead an ANC activist named Chris Hani using a gun loaned to him by a **conservative** politician. Mandela made a powerful speech in which he called on all South Africans to "stand together."

After Hani's death, the ANC and the government returned to negotiations. They soon announced that South Africa's first full democratic elections would take place in April 1994. Apartheid was over. For their efforts, Mandela and de Klerk were jointly awarded the Nobel Prize for Peace in 1993.

ELECTED PRESIDENT

On April 26, 1994, more than 22 million South Africans voted. Many stood in line for hours to cast their vote. The ANC won easily, and Mandela became the first black president of South Africa.

The office of the President of South Africa is in the Union Buildings in Pretoria.

Mandela presented the world cup trophy to François Pienaar, captain of South Africa's victorious rugby team.

De Klerk became one of his deputies in what Mandela called the Government of National Unity. The new president said he wanted to create "a rainbow nation at peace with itself and the world."

Mandela decided to use sports to unify the country. After years of isolation, when other countries refused to play there, South Africa hosted the Rugby World Cup in 1995. Rugby was seen as a sport of the white minority, and few blacks supported it. Now Mandela encouraged all South Africans to rally around the national team. He attended the final in a public show of support for the team. South Africa won the cup in a victory that helped bring the country together.

INTRODUCING CHANGE

To help heal the country's divisions, Mandela also set up what he called the Truth and Reconciliation Commission to investigate crimes and violations of human rights by both sides in the previous 34 years. He introduced a new economic plan to create jobs for poor blacks, as well as providing health care and better housing. In 1996, Mandela introduced a new **constitution** for South Africa. The constitution set up a strong central government while ensuring that the black majority would have the strongest say in any democratic elections.

As president, Mandela encouraged new housing programs for poor black South Africans.

Thabo Mbeki meets Chancellor Angela Merkel of Germany. Mbeki replaced Mandela in 1999 and remained president until 2008.

The constitution also guaranteed the rights of all minority groups—including the whites who formerly governed the country. De Klerk's National Party opposed the constitution, and withdrew from the government.

STANDING DOWN

By 1999, Mandela had overseen the **transition** of South Africa from white minority rule to full democracy. On his 80th birthday the previous year, he had married his third wife, the humanitarian Graça Machel. Mandela was ready to retire. At the end of his term as president, he stepped down in favor of his deputy in the ANC, Thabo Mbeki.

Mandela's FAMILY LIFE

Nelson Mandela gave up a normal family life to devote himself to the struggle for civil rights. His family had to do the same.

Mandela was married three times and had a total of six children. Mandela's status meant that his children and even his grandchildren became well known in South African life. For much of the early part of his children's lives, however, Mandela was an absent father. He was either touring the country campaigning for the ANC or in prison.

Mandela married his first wife, Evelyn, in 1944. They had two sons and two daughters, one of whom died in infancy. The couple were divorced in 1958. They grew apart because of Mandela's political work.

Evelyn Mase became frustrated that Mandela spent so much time on politics rather than his family.

Winnie Mandela (third from right) attends a funeral of an ANC leader. She remained active in politics after her marriage to Mandela ended in 1996.

In 1958, Mandela married Winnie Madikizela. She was an ANC activist. While her husband was in prison, she raised their two daughters, Zenani and Zindziswa. She also became a prominent campaigner in the continuing struggle against apartheid. Mandela and Winnie were divorced in 1996.

On his 80th birthday in 1998, Mandela married for a third time. His new wife was Graça Machel. She was the widow of Samora Machel, the president of Mozambique. Graça Machel has a reputation as an international **humanitarian** campaigner who supports women's and children's rights.

Nelson and Winnie Mandela arrive in Washington, DC, in 1990, the year he was released from prison.

Global SYMBOL

When Mandela quit politics, he was one of the most admired figures in the world for his efforts to overcome racism in South Africa.

Even after he retired, Mandela's reputation continued to grow. As a mark of respect, many South Africans began to refer to him by his clan name, Madiba. He became a leading supporter of human rights and peaceful social change around the world. With his gray hair and colorful "Madiba" shirts, he was an easily recognizable figure. However, after all the optimism of South Africa's first democratic elections and the administration of the first black president, it became clear that, despite Mandela's efforts in office, South Africa still faced many problems.

QUICK FACTS

- After his presidency ended, Nelson remained a high-profile campaigner.
- His death caused an outpouring of grief around the world.

Some black South Africans were frustrated by the slow speed of change in areas such as housing.

GROWING CRITICISM

Some black voters had been disappointed by Mandela's failure to introduce quicker reform of jobs and housing. Crime levels were high, particularly in the townships where many black South Africans lived. In addition, Mandela also found his efforts to act fairly for everyone undermined by the actions of other ANC leaders. Critics accused many of these other politicians of being **corrupt**. The targets of criticism included Mandela's former wife, Winnie, who remained a high-profile politician after the couple divorced in 1996. Winnie Mandela was later found guilty of fraud and theft, and sentenced to five years in jail.

At the same time, political chaos had begun to harm South Africa's neighbors, including Lesotho and Zimbabwe, but Mandela had done little. He was also slow to react to an outbreak of human immunodeficiency virus/acquired immune deficiency syndrome (HIV/AIDS) in South Africa. The fatal disease is spread by sexual contact or by blood transfusions.

A QUIET RETIREMENT

Despite such problems, Mandela left office with a high reputation. More than 80 percent of all South Africans judged him a successful president. He planned to spend his retirement quietly. He wanted to divide his time between Johannesburg and his home in Qunu. Instead, he found he was still involved in politics.

As president, Thabo Mbeki faced many of the same problems as Mandela.

In 1999, Mandela founded the Nelson Mandela Foundation. This charity aimed to tackle what he had come to see as the basic problems affecting black South Africans. These were rural poverty, a lack of schools, and the fight against HIV/AIDS.

TACKLING HIV/AIDS

Now that he was out of office, Mandela led the campaign to use education and drugs to try to prevent the spread of HIV/AIDS. Between 2003 and 2008, the organization 46664—named for Mandela's prisoner number—set up pop concerts in South Africa and Europe to raise money to fight against AIDS. In a cruel blow, Mandela's son Makgatho died of the diease in 2005.

The Nelson Mandela Foundation made creating new schools a priority.

This stamp celebrates Mandela receiving an honor in Australia in 1999. His reputation remained high around the world.

ANOTHER RETIREMENT

In 2004, Mandela decided his ill health meant he needed to do less work. He announced that he was "retiring from retirement." In a farewell speech to his fellow South Africans, he asked to be left alone, saying, "Don't call me, I'll call you."

Still, however, he continued to travel widely and to meet with world leaders such as President George W. Bush and Senator Barack Obama, who later became U.S. president himself. In 2007, Mandela announced the formation of a group called The Elders. These were senior former international leaders from around the world. Mandela believed they could help behind the scenes in international disputes by encouraging communication and helping to avoid conflict.

FINAL APPEARANCE

Mandela's last public appearance came during the soccer World Cup in 2010. He had campaigned for the event to be held in South Africa, and now he made a rare appearance at the final. He was given a hero's welcome by the huge crowd. The event reminded people of the Rugby World Cup of 1995.

In 2009, the story of the Rugby World Cup had been told in a successful Hollywood movie. In *Invictus*, Morgan Freeman played Mandela. In 2013, he was the subject of another movie. *Long Walk to Freedom* was based on an **autobiography** he wrote in 1995. This time, Idris Elba played Mandela.

South Africans support the national team during the 2010 soccer World Cup.

Flowers surround a statue of Mandela in London, UK, after his death in 2013.

GLOBAL GRIEF

From 2011 onward, Mandela began to suffer from problems with his lungs, which prevented him from breathing properly. He spent time in the hospital as his health continued to fail. Finally, on December 5, 2013, he died, aged 95.

South Africa marked the death of the former president with 10 days of national mourning. Mandela's state funeral was attended by many international political leaders. Newspapers and broadcasters around the world paid tribute to the man who had helped to end apartheid and steered South Africa into a new age of democracy and racial equality. Mandela once said that he had been fighting racial discrimination his whole life and would fight it until the day he died. Many people believed he had done just that.

Timeline

1918	• Born and named Rolihlahla Mandela on July 18.
1930	• On the death of his father, he is taken to be raised by the regent of the Thembu people.
1939	• Enrolls at University College of Fort Hare in Alice.
1940	• Is expelled and soon runs away to Johannesburg.
1943	• Enrolls to study law at the University of Witwatersrand.
1944	• Helps start the ANC Youth League with Oliver Tambo; marries Evelyn Mase.
1952	• Is sentenced to nine months in prison, though the sentence is suspended. With Tambo, he opens South Africa's first black law firm, Mandela & Tambo.
1956	• Is arrested and charged with high treason with 155 other ANC leaders.
1958	• Divorces Evelyn Mase and marries Winnie Madikizela.
1960	• The Sharpeville Massacre; ANC is banned.
1961	• Secretly organizes a three-day strike; forms Umkhonto we Sizwe and becomes its commander in chief.
1962	• Leaves the country to raise support for the armed struggle. On his return, he is arrested and sentenced to five years in prison.
1963	• Joins nine other ANC leaders on trial for sabotage in the Rivonia Trial.

1964	• Is sentenced with seven others to life imprisonment.
1986	• Starts meetings to persuade the government to talk to the ANC.
1990	• Is released from prison, and leads the ANC delegation in talks with the government.
1993	• Wins the Nobel Peace Prize jointly with President F. W. de Klerk.
1994	• Votes in South Africa's first democratic election and becomes president; publishes his autobiography, *Long Walk to Freedom*.
1999	• Steps down after only one term as president; starts the Nelson Mandela Foundation.
2003	• Founds the 46664 campaign to highlight HIV and AIDS.
2004	• Retires from politics, saying, "Don't call me, I'll call you."
2009	• Nelson Mandela International Day is proclaimed by the United Nations.
2013	• Dies at his home in Johannesburg, aged 95; is given a state funeral.

KEY PUBLICATIONS

- *Long Walk to Freedom* (1994)
- *Conversations with Myself* (2010)
- *Nelson Mandela by Himself: The Authorized Book of Quotations* (2014)

Glossary

apartheid A legal system based on keeping races apart.

autobiography A written account of someone's own life.

boycotts Refusing to buy goods as a political protest.

civil disobedience Peacefully refusing to obey unjust laws.

civil rights People's right to social and political freedom.

clan A large group of families that are related to one another.

colony A region ruled by another country.

conservative Against political change.

constitution A set of guidelines for governing a country.

corrupt Acting dishonestly in return for personal gain.

discrimination Unfair treatment of a group of people.

figurehead A recognizable leader of a group or movement.

guerrilla Someone who fights using methods such as surprise attacks or killings.

humanitarian Trying to improve human well-being.

missionaries People who try to spread a religion.

pass books Official documents that allowed non-white South Africans to travel around.

prejudice Hostility toward someone based on their race, sex, or other factors.

racist Believing that one race is superior to others.

radical Extreme.

regent Someone who rules in place of a king or queen.

sabotage The destruction of property.

segregated Kept separate on the basis of race or other factors.

shanty towns Settlements of small, poorly built huts.

symbolic Standing for something important.

township A suburb in South Africa for black residents.

transition A change from one situation to another.

Further Resources

Books

Bundy, Colin. *Nelson Mandela.* History Makers. New York: Cavendish Square, 2016.

Mandela, Nelson. *Long Walk to Freedom (abridged edition).* London: Macmillan Children's Books, 2005.

Meyer, Susan. *Nelson Mandela: South African President and Anti-Apartheid Activist.* Spotlight on Civic Courage. New York City: Rosen Young Adult, 2017.

Nelson, Kristen Rajczak. *Nelson Mandela.* Heroes of Black History. New York: Gareth Stevens, 2015.

Websites

Apartheid
history.howstuffworks.com/historical-events/apartheid.htm
A page about apartheid and South Africa's racist history.

Nelson Mandela
www.natgeokids.com/uk/discover/history/general-history/nelson-mandela/
A biography of Nelson Mandela and his achievements.

Nelson Mandela Foundation
www.nelsonmandela.org
The website of the foundation, with details of its many activities.

Timeline
www.nelsonmandela.org/content/page/learners-timeline
A detailed timeline about Nelson Mandela's life.

Publisher's note to educators and parents: Our editors have carefully reviewed these websites to ensure that they are suitable for students. Many websites change frequently, however, and we cannot guarantee that a site's future contents will continue to meet our high standards of quality and educational value. Be advised that students should be closely supervised whenever they access the Internet.

Index